Skinny Beni

"Incidents and Happenings

Also By The Author

Skinny Beni
"'One Wing Out"

Skinny Beni
"Fiercely Runny Roommate Stores and Pet
Padandories"

Skinny Beni
"A-Go-Go"

and

Girls Like ME

Skinny Beni Incidence and Happenings

Copyright@2015 by BJ Davis

Printed in the United States of America. All rights
reserved.

ISBN: 978-1-936748-66-2

Skinny Beni
Incidents and Happenings

Created by BJ Davis
Sketching Madness by Lidia Churakova

Dedication of Appreciation

Thank you Loretta Myers! You taught me how to appreciate the value of reading a great book, the art of laughing at life's drama, love for bands like Fleetwood Mac and the willingness to at least try to spell things correctly.

I adore you!

And to my sister, Karen Kelly, who always got my kind of silliness.

Acknowledgement

I salute all the fun people who had a hand in breathing life into Skinny Beni...

Ann Jagger, you are an amazing author, producer, writing coach. Thanks for laughing all the time at my work. Gaylene Schaffer, my mom, who didn't approve of some of the language but closed one eye and forge ahead to help edit and "suggest" changes. To my daughter Kaysha who supported this writing ambition. Scott Markowitz, my friend and creative coach who just happens to be an award winning photographer and videographer and who shot the recent footage for Skinny Beni. And to Yesenia Bocanegra who shot and edited (impeccably) the first round of footage before I went grey! (Writing a book has taken its toll) and to all my neighbors and friends who volunteered to randomly read my work while being filmed and to the complete strangers in downtown Raleigh, NC who were caught off guard when coerced into reading the work of Skinny Beni and allowing themselves to be filmed! My hat's off to the array of musical talent; Cat Albanese (Popcorn Wings! You are a Genius), and Tom Miller your hubby and sidekick that edited and produced that song for me!. And to all the creative illustrators, Kay Parks, Ellie Bonifant, and Lidia Churakova who finalized our current Skinny Beni images in this book. I thank you all and appreciate your gifts and talents so very very much!

A glimpse of things to come...

It is as crisp a memory as the winter air that orchestrated the knocking of my uncovered knees.

I'm sitting sardined with a dozen other children from my nursery school in the back of a pickup truck made into a parade float.

We are slowly moving towards a crowd of people lined up on each side of the street whom I am sure are anxiously waiting to wave back at my 4-year-old face.

At first, I didn't recognize the crazy screaming person running behind us. The object she is holding high above her head is flapping in the cold wind. My first thought was that she is part of the show.

She jumps up into the back of the truck scaring the crap out of me and the other human popsicles. The truck halts completely in the middle of the parade route.

"Beni put these on." I pretended like I don't know her, so she will go away. She doesn't!

She holds up the leotards and motions me to walk over. She now publicly assists me in getting dressed in front of all my fans.

The rest of the memory blurs off, but I do remember someone saying, "look at her skinny little legs."

Branded henceforth as "Skinny Beni," this would be the first of many public displays. Most self-induced!

The Skinny Beni series is a hodgepodge of odd, funny, silly, and sometimes sad (not too many of them) incidents and happenings captured in print.

Skinny Beni books are an excellent read when you want to check out and ignore everything around you, especially screaming kids, delayed flights, OB GYN checkups, mandatory update classes to keep your Real Estate licenses, etc.

Unexpectedly, people fall in love with Skinny Beni all the time in the weirdest places and for even weirder reasons, so I am told.

I hope you have as much fun reading these books and reflecting on your own cosmic induced silliness as I did writing them.

Smiles and hugs,

BJ Davis, aka Skinny Beni

All of life could be summed up in three words:

incidents and happenings

Incidents

I don't like a man who thinks
he is funnier than me.
How annoyingly
Unattractive!

Eavesdropping

"Chris won't be coming home till spring," she chirps. "I've got some time to lose these extra pounds."

The reflection in the mirror smiles back while continuously dabbing color from paint brush to hair strands. "You'll lose it," she says encouragingly.

"Did you hear about Rebecca?"

"Rebecca Milton?"

"That's her. Rumor has it she's three months pregnant."

"No way, she has two already!"

"Yep! Get this, her husband's been serving overseas for 5 months!" "You do the math."

The reflection's eyes go wide. Painted-hair girl smiles wickedly.

"Ok, back to the rinse bowl for you," orders my stylist.

Ears burning, I am annoyed at being pulled away from the drama climaxing in the chair next to me.

Happenings

Grits.
You don't like grits?
On what planet
is that even possible?

Bring It Back

Let's bring "groovy" back!
I'd say it's just about time
for us to chill on out,
step away from the daily grind.
So, let's bring "groovy" back,
let the word tumble from our lips,
All that anger and drama
100% <u>Not hip</u>!!!!!

Incidents

Have you ever noticed how many times people will continue to push the elevator button even though it's already lit?

Cracks me up every time!

Richard Cranium

Hello I'm Richard Cranium. I believe we've met before.

Just stopping by to say hi as I'm headed out the door.

Richard Cranium? Yes, I've known a few.

So, let me think for a minute where I might have met you.

You kind of look like and I believe you

just might be, the Richard Cranium

who once ran into me!

Never did he claim what obviously

was his fault, when he ran that stop sign

and refused his car to halt

Or could you be that Richard with that same last name, who sold me a clunker, you should be ashamed!

Or maybe you're the one I dated for a while. Snappy dresser, white teeth. My OH my. You had such style!

You now got me thinking, though I've tried hard to forget...

All the Richard Craniums I have ever met

The one that tried to sell me some timeshare, just came to mind, His fake smile soon faded, when I refused to sign

O yes, you're right.

We've met many times before.

Different face. Different place.

So, you can keep moving towards that door!

If there's one thing I've learned,

and I believe it's true.

Your nickname, "d*#K head," really suits you!

Smarty Pants

I can't stand Smarty Pants People!

You know the one.

Always raising their hand.

Postponing break time.

Cutting into pre-test review time.

Delaying early - release so you're not caught
in the rush hour traffic.

Dang you Smarty Pants!

Counting Off

One, Two
where are my shoes?
Three, Four
I creep out the door
Five, Six
I'm tired of dating pricks
Seven, Eight
in bed, he's great
Nine, Ten
I'm counting off again

Poof

I call my mother, we chit and chatter
I can't get her off the phone
The guilt is rising, her warning advising
to call my sisters before long
You know Beni one day they'll all go away
The Lord calls everyone home
I'm so busy right now, I say and then frown
My heartstrings she tugs with her tone
Someday you'll look back, she says,
with a fact
I assure you it won't be that long
The call you don't place, will never erase
the quietness when "poof"
they're gone!

Happenings

Do you want to know how I found out that
I'm not really that patient?

I don't fare well with compulsive channel
clickers!

You know the person.

The one that says,

"Hey, do you mind if I see what else is on?"

Click. Click. Click.

Waitressing Tips

Shortly after my divorce, I found myself in a financial dilemma. It was a hard winter and as a Realtor I was starving in a slow market.

Wanting to be proactive, I decided to take a waitressing job a couple of nights a week.

Sharing this new strategy with my mom, she could not resist the opportunity to help me make the most of my new side-career.

"Beni, I know you're gonna think I'm crazy when I say this, but I have some waitressing advice for you."

Holding my breath, a learned behavior from childhood, my heart races like it's running away from something terrifying whenever my mom is about to share her wisdom.

Her advice is often delivered with some raw southern logic that comes out of nowhere. I'm always hard-pressed to think anyone, even my mom, would have the inclination to follow it.

Still thinking in my head; when was my mother ever a waitress, she seizes the moment to spill her logic as if my pause has constituted an agreement for her to continue.

"Don't lay your crotch on the table!" she states.

That was it! That was the advice!

This, from the woman who had laden my childhood with whimsical quips of parenting logic such as, "don't eat your boogers, you'll get worms in your underpants," came "don't lay your crotch on the table."

I was stunned and silent.

"Beni, I'm serious."

I had no doubt she was.

"Women do it all the time when they're taking an order," she affirmed, "they'll move too close to the corner of the table, and there you have it!"

I'm not sure how the call ended.

With most conversations with my mother, I'm often left a little confused about how life really works.

I store most of her logic way back in the cramped attic of my brain and pull it down occasionally for weird teachable moments with my own daughter.

Even after the shock past from this verbal exchange, I have caught myself now and then looking at waitresses' crotches when they take my order.

It is an odd moment for both of us.

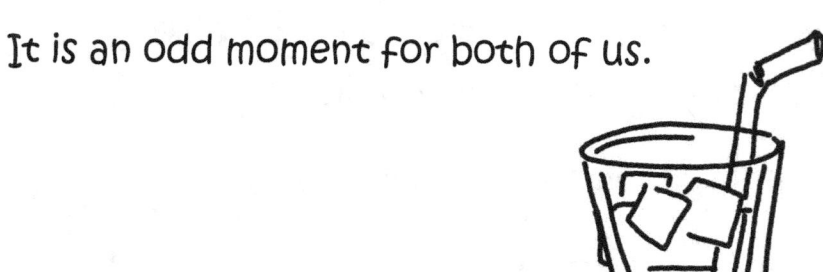

Incidents

Kiss.
Don't kiss.
I hate that odd moment
at the end of
the first date.

Happenings

Warning.
Taking herb pills will
make your armpits
stink out loud!

Our First Time

I wish I could have worn a different gown.

It didn't seem to matter to you.

"Relax and lay back," your eyes and voice were so reassuring.

I tried not letting my anxiousness overtake me.

I followed your directions and put my arm behind my head, the same position I used when stargazing.

Your hands, so thorough, moved as though they were searching for something.

What a touch-fest for my heaving bosoms.

Knees clenched, you beckoned me with soft words of assurance.

I let them fall open as you guided my legs into position.

"All done," you exclaimed!

I released the trapped air I was holding inside.

I smiled.

You smiled back.

"We'll see you in a year."

"Go ahead and get dressed," you instructed, "I'll send the nurse in for some follow-up instructions."

My, what a charmer you are!

Bummer

I'm in First Grade

the smallest girl in the class

I get to stand next to Troy Bilskie, the shortest boy in the class.

Bummer

I'm in the Third Grade

the slowest runner in the class

Troy Bilskie always tags me first in recess.

Bummer

I'm in the Fifth Grade

best friends with the prettiest girl in the class

Troy Bilskie is in love with her.

Bummer

Happenings

I wish I didn't have such a caring
loving face that says,
"Why, I would love to talk about
the last five women you were in
a relationship with..."

Incidents

It's a real struggle for me at times to
focus on what
someone else is saying.
Especially when distracted by
something interesting
going on <u>right behind them</u>!

Shipwrecked

Menopause. Menopause.

Nothing pauses in Menopause.

Hormones are screaming,

sometimes out loud,

0 to 90--instant witch--I'm not proud!

Menopause. Menopause.

No, nothing pauses in menopause.

Breast drooping, vagina drying.

Overreacting and then crying!

My mind I've lost.

Sleepless nights, I just toss.

Gorging on chocolate, just because.

I'm shipwrecked on the island of
menopause!

Happenings

I could nibble at fried chicken crust
all day long without ever
eating a whole piece!

Incidents

It's very hard not to
steal a fry
from someone else's plate
while they're gone
to fetch ketchup.

Pancake Blankets

Wrap me up in pancake blankets
all the way from toes to snout.
Warm and cuddly.
Soft and snuggly.
I'll nibble my way right out!
Wrap me up in pancake blankets
and forgive my buttery chin.
I'll sit in my chair
throw my feet in the air
kicking marshmallow-shoes off
with a grin!

Love Sick

Thump. Thump.
What's that feeling?
Thump. Thump.
My heart Is reeling
Thump. Thump.
I'm just healing
and I'm not willing
to get "love-sick" today!

Happenings

Help!
My bladder has fallen
and it
can't get up!

Gravity

I look in the mirror
and what do I see?
The drooping boobs your
handy-work has gifted me!
My necks' all wrinkly, my butt's sliding off
I look like a rhino
drinking straight from a trough.
O yes, please tell me what did I do
to make you defy me, I haven't a clue!

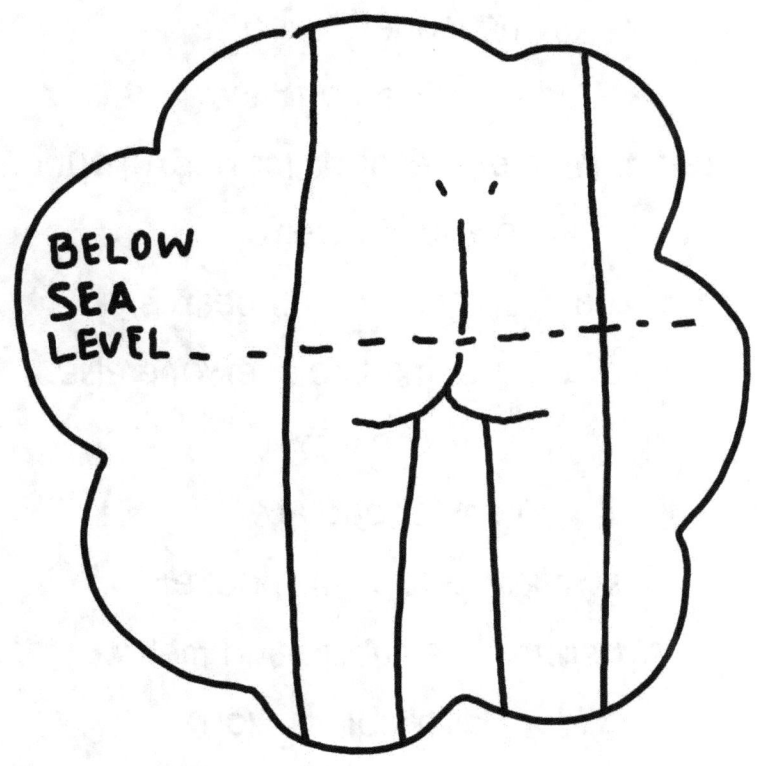

Quirky

You seem surprised
when I've rationalized
whether to buy by the ounce or the pound
"Saving money?", you say
I know it's an odd way
there are simpler methods more profound.
To you it's weird
that I shave my chin beard
instead of plucking like everyone else.
Or the way
I eat chocolate
straight out of my pocket
as it stains the fabric and melts.
No, I don't blame you
I would refrain too
witnessing my odd behaviors and quirks,
but I might surprise you
my life you don't blow through realizing
it's just the way my brain works!

Incidents

What's that racket on the radio
they are calling music these days?
Most importantly,
how did my grandma's voice
get inside my head???

Happenings

Do you know how to tell
that he's not a
"great guy?"
When he keeps repeatedly
telling you that
he's a "great guy!"

High Expectations

Tossed back into the dating world, finding a decent guy to date has become encumbering and mentally taxing!

It's like having a second full-time job while training for a triathlon.

Am I wrong ladies?

I've filled out more survey questions that would topple all my essay writings over the span of four years in college.

There's nothing that I haven't shared about myself.

From favorite pastimes, religious beliefs or un-beliefs, what food I'm most likely to want to eat on a first date, I covered it all!

I've taken my time to describe in much detail the kind of man I am looking for. I'm beginning to wonder if I set my expectations way too high.

What I Said I Want	What Wants Me
Middle-Aged Professional	Old Geezer Named Bubba or Rocky.
Educated	Knows People Who Can Get Stuff
Physically Fit	Openly Admits to Being a Hefty Eater and Pictures Don't Lie
Family Focused	Loves His Momma, Lives with His Momma
Likes to Travel	Can't Wait for the State Fair
Non-smoker	Smokes Pot Occasionally, Meaning All the Time!
Likes to Dance	Likes to Go to Strip Clubs and Watch
Spiritual	Can't Stop Saying, "God you're beautiful. I can't wait to see you neck-ed."

The Downside of Laughter

What's the matter?

I've lost control of my bladder.

Every time I laugh I pee!

All serious now, sporting a frown,

denying the "Depends" I need.

What's the problem?

You say, so solemn, as liquid runs

down my knees

"OH, I don't know...

(avoiding a show)

I run off to find dry panties.

Incidents

I've become the lunatic
on the dance floor
thinking she has
all the cool
moves!

Riddle Me This

When I was thinner
I was a winner
even the boys thought so.
When I was slimmer
my clothes would glimmer
it didn't seem that long ago.
But now I'm fat!
What's up with that?
I think, while eating popcorn
and watching my shows.

Happenings

I love to try other people's food choices.

I will purposely order something

different just so I can

ask for a bite.

Sick behavior.

I know!

Sorry I'm Late

I was just about to step out the door to meet you when I saw an email come in.

Seeing that it was something I could answer in a couple of words I sat down to send a quick reply.

Realizing I had been sitting all day I reached to pull out my stand-up desk and noticed the gross amount of cat hair that had accumulated there.

Disgusted, I grabbed the broom and gave it a couple of swipes.

Broom in hand I quickly remembered the mounting pile of fall leaves invading my back door and seized the moment to rid myself of the unwanted debris.

Looking down from the porch, I noticed a dog toy that didn't belong outside. Irritated at my four-legged friend, I fetched the toy.

Refocusing, I turned to climb the stairs back into the house. Glancing down I saw the weeds that needed my immediate attention and thank God I had planned so carefully to leave early; there was still time to pull these "beasts of burden" and rid them from my life!

Job well done. I couldn't believe the amount of dirt that had collected under my fingernails from this simple task.

A good scrubbing was in order. Armed with the nail brush I scrubbed and scrubbed while glancing out the kitchen window.

Seeing my neighbor's trash can, I realized I had forgotten to set mine out.

Making a quick run through the house, I gathered the garbage and wheeled it out to the curve.

Throwing my stuff in the car and speeding like crazy to get here without killing myself, I glanced into the rearview mirror.

Pulling over I applied a couple of layers of eyeliner and mascara to make my lashes look full and my eyes bigger. I wanted to look my best for you.

Again, thanks for waiting!

So, what were we meeting about?

Savvy

"Right click!"

She clicks left.

"Don't use the back arrow, it will take

you out of the site."

Long pause.

A true indicator that she has left the site.

"Save before you close!"

Click!

Oops.

Heat travels towards my <u>last</u>

frazzled nerve.

"We can start again tomorrow, I say."

"I guess I'm not that good at this

computer stuff."

"No, you're not, but you sure

got that clicking thing down!"

Incidents

My gym sells protein bars with

23 grams of sugar

37 grams of carbs

and...

550 calories!

What a great way to insure long-term

Clientele.

More Like Her. Less Like Me!

I have this other person that shares the same body as I do.

She's put me in a pickle a time or two because I truly didn't know what she was going to say.

I have been caught off guard explaining "what she meant by that," while she regresses back inside this space we share.

She speaks her mind. Clear and precise.

Some nerve.

It's crazy.

Unlike her, I fumble for words which is ok I guess except that there are times the right ones would help tilt the conversation back to center and away from awkward.

She's witty this strong-ness inside me.

Inquisitive. Firm. Analytical.

I'm in awe of her and yet afraid of her all in the same thought.

She's just soo together.

She goes by the name Confidence.

Go figure!

Happenings

What doesn't turn me on you ask?
Being stabbed twice in the ankle by the
same scary, overgrown toenail
I suggested he trim earlier!

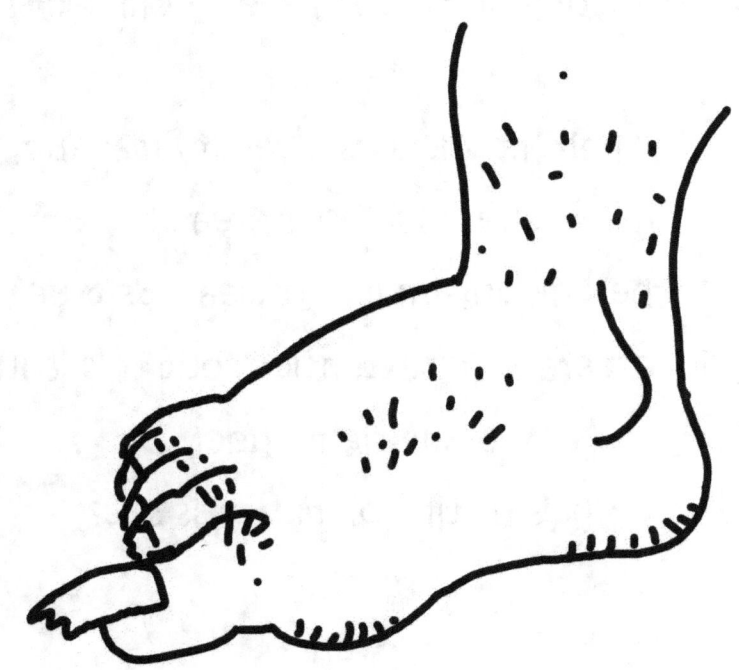

Flirting!!

She's hitting on me, and it's causing
quite a stir.
I've seen her around, but her name is
a blur.
She's hitting on me with every comment she
makes.
My hair, my clothes, even my makeup,
she says, looks great!
She's hitting on me, I swear it's true
I'm desperate for attention, but this is just
down right rude!
She's hitting on me, or is she?
I rethink...
Crap!
She's the makeover artist I hired,
Man, she looks amazing in pink!

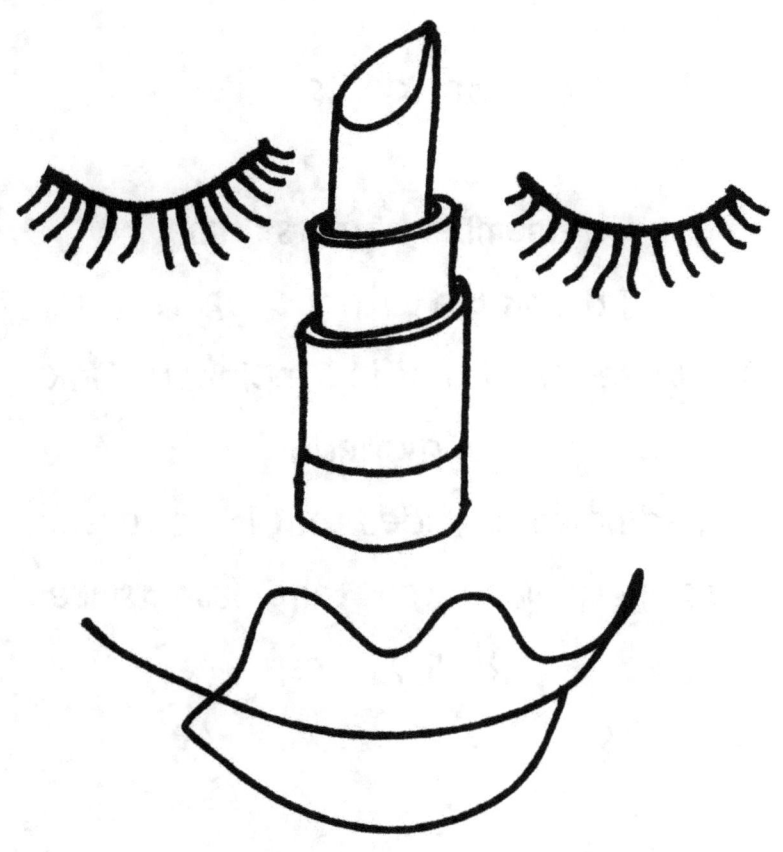

Incidents

I remember the first time
I drank tea without sugar.
I sat in a restaurant in Cincinnati, Ohio
and cried!
I had no earthly idea that it was even
possible to make "tea" that wasn't sweet.
Reality Bites!

Note to Self

Today I will

Head in the direction of where my feet are pointed.

which is forwards

Today I will

Let go of anything that is out of my control.

Claiming power only over my thoughts and actions!

Today I will

Refuse to be enslaved by should've, would've, could've.

Declaring them all a waste of time and brainpower

Today I will

Move to the rhythm of my own dance.

Stepping, when I'm ready, both backwards and forwards...

And when it's time to change the music

Today I will

Happenings

I'm always so excited when the
weekend rolls around.
I can't wait to go out and kick up my heels
and do something exciting and fun!
Never fails.
7:00 pm I'm yawning
and ready for bed.

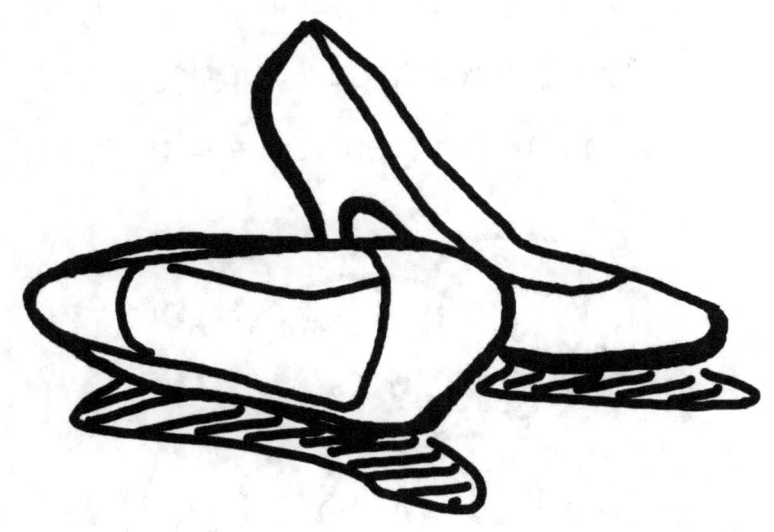

These Theys'

Who are these "theys" that say so much?

We use their curbside wisdom,

a terrible verbal crutch!

Advice about everything

"they" seem to know.

Love. War. Parenting.

The list just grows!

I've never met these "theys,"

I honestly admit.

But I catch myself quoting

they're constant bull#@it!

Incidents

I love making a meal out of
in-store samples.
It takes a lot of time and slick
maneuvers to look like
you're shopping while grazing.

The Perfect Fit

"I hate bra shopping!"

I announced this to the two women behind the counter. Both heads snapped up. I said it louder than intended.

"Which one of you is the expert on bra fitting?" I demanded.

"Stacy," the older woman chided. Using her head as a directional arrow she motioned towards her co-worker.

Without hesitation, Stacy looped a measuring tape around her neck and trotted off towards the back of the store.

"Are you coming?" she asked, as though it was the most natural thing for me to do; follow a stranger into a dressing room.

I followed.

Stacy shut the door behind us.

She wasted no time getting up in my personal space.

Raise your arms. Higher! "Yep, looks like you're a double D. It could be because of the sweater," she explained.

"Double D?" I blurted!

"I mean I know I've gained some weight and...,"

"Follow me," she ordered.

Opening the door, she was on a mission, and with laser focus went right towards the expensive bras I had avoided earlier.

"Here, try this on."

"Oh no," I replied," I don't do lace, it itches and looks bumpy under my shirts."

I demonstrated how I might rub itchy breasts.

She watched and waited until I was done.

"Yep I hear that a lot and I'm telling you you're going to be surprised how this looks and feels."

She sternly handed me the bra. There would be no choices.

"OH Ok, well I will just ummm try this on..."

I turned in the direction of the dressing room we had ascended from.

I would lose her at the next bra rack and go back hunting the bra beast in the sales bin by myself.

"Where are you going?" she barked.

"In here, let's try it on," she pointed towards the dressing room.

Stunned, I succumbed to her authority and walked back into the room where we had started.

I turned to close the door behind me, unaware that Stacy had magically slipped in. She would be staying for the fitting.

"Take off your shirt and turn around."

"What?"

"Take off your shirt and turn around so I can put this on you."

I hadn't had anyone help me put on a bra since the age of 10.

"OK," I replied, in a ten-year-old voice.

Over the head and looped around my arms, Stacy guided the new bra onto my chest with a pair of mother-nurturing hands.

"Now see how nice that looks?" She beamed with pride.

"Oh my," I exclaimed! "My girls look perky and smaller; I love this bra, I squealed!

"Now why don't you grab that new shirt I see hanging out of your bag there, and let's see how it looks on," she suggested.

Moving with the speed of presents being unwrapped Christmas morning, I pulled the new blouse over my head and turning around faced the mirror.

I couldn't believe how nice my breasts looked in the new shirt.

I felt younger, prettier.

Gazing in the mirror, I smiled.

My eyes traveled from my chest to the reflection in the mirror right behind me. There was Stacy, with a look of contentment on her face.

I couldn't help but think I had made her proud. So very proud!

Swimming

"I see this as growth," you say.

"I do too!" I lie.

Eyes sting.

Ears ring.

Heart heavy as a brick

"We make better friends," you claim

"Of course!" I reply.

Dry mouth.

Hoarse voice.

Numb mind.

"You'll find someone perfect," you affirm.

'You too!" I smile.

It's exhausting swimming to

the other side of you.

Happenings

Whom among us is strong enough
to resist a box of thin mints.
Especially when it's being
"pimped" by a third grader, sporting
pigtails!

Wall Décor

Image plastered on the wall
who's that woman standing all nice and tall?
Shoulders held back and chin tilted high
Perky breasts that point towards the sky
Teeth that sparkle, straight as can be
No, she's not real, she's a poster you see
A model that's molded and perfectly made
Blonde hair, blue eyes--a soft aqua shade
No, she's not real, and I know not why
I want to be her
I think and then sigh

Request

I want to go out frazzled
worn through and through.
Not an ounce of life left in me
nothing more left to do.
I want to go out tattered
a life thoroughly spent.
My pockets turned inside out
revealing not one last cent!

Incidents

I can officially say I'm wearing
"big girl panties"
Also known as
"Granny Panties."

So Gross

Booger Picker Booger Picker

Can'test thou see,

you're picking your nose in the car

next to me.

Booger Picker Booger Picker

Please stop. Seriously stop!

You're going to force my hand

and I'll call the Booger Pick'n Cops.

Booger Picker Booger Picker,

I would certainly drive away.

The traffic's backed up so beside you

I'll stay.

Booger Picker Booger Picker

Seriously?

I CAN SEE YOU OUT OF THE CORNER
OF MY EYE AND SO CAN
<u>EVERYONE ELSE!</u>

You've totally ruined my Dorito binging.

I'm so grossed out!

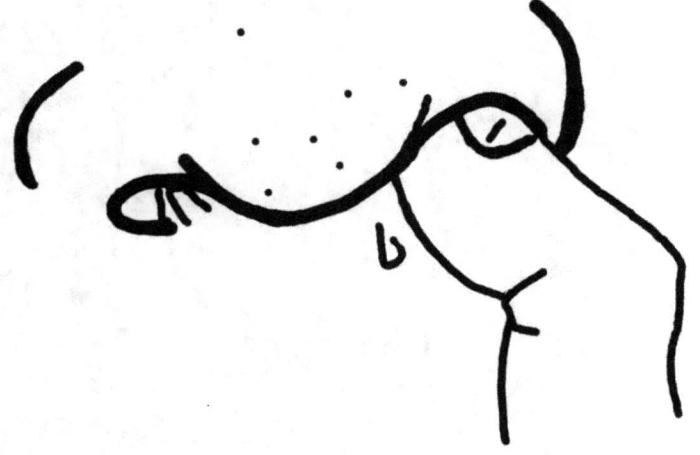

Happenings

Heavy sweaters...
suffocate me!

Mirror, Mirror on the Floor

I can't bear to look!

Apparently, men rate vaginas as sometimes ugly.

I'm curious to find out if mine is.

I call my girlfriend Leana,

She's curious too.

I swear I cannot tell.

I call my ex-husband.

Ring. Ring.

"Hey, got a question for you."

He does not respond.

"Do you think I have an ugly vagina?"

Long pause.

"It did what it was supposed to do," he states.

"Stop calling me with weird ass questions!"

And then he hung up.

Incidents

I must sleep with a pillow between my knees.

If I can't find a pillow,

I will put any random object there in its place.

It's an odd way to wake up.

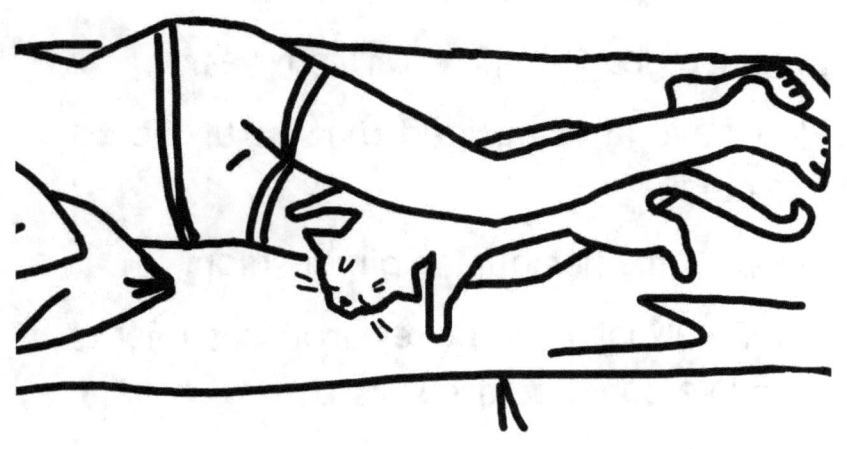

The Fall Out

Invisible tension tethers between she and I.

I look at her for any sign that she is aware. She seems not to be.

Her forced laughter annoys me.

Everything she says seems pretentious, ill-suited for the situations being rolled out in our "girls' weekend" away.

We have been friends for many years.

How have I not noticed that I truly do not like her?

I've become her human pin cushion.

She freely jabs and pokes around subjects that I've confided are sensitive.

She performs this ritual in front of other women she calls friends.

My heart burns.

I search through years of familiarity to find a single strand that has not snapped away from the relationship we have shared.

There is none.

The thought saddens me, and I know, and maybe in her eyes I can see that she knows too...

we are no longer friends, she and I.

Mind Straw

Rumpelstiltskin.

Rumpelstiltskin

Wherefore art thou Rumpelstiltskin?

My mind is mush.

The work piles up.

I have been appointed "Commander and Chief" over all these great ideas I've conjured up.

Everyone parades around my enthusiasm and creativity.

Sentenced to a desk that has become a prison of endless papers, sticky notes, folders, and postcards, I have come to the realization I cannot spin all this mind-straw into gold!

Rumpelstiltskin?

Where is that little angry man when you need him?

Two Girls Laughing

It had been awhile since they had seen each other.

I wondered if there would be any awkwardness that time and distance can create between childhood friends.

From the second they locked eyes and hearts at baggage claim, my daughter and her best friend were back among the familiar.

Time fell away on embrace.

Glancing in the rearview, I had to smile at the scene of them sharing their lives at rapid speed.

One listening and nodding. The other chatting and making big arm gestures.

OH, how I had missed the sweetness their friendship brought to everything.

Once home, bags were dropped at the front door.

Off the two trotted, locked arm-n-arm, back into a world they purposely created for themselves so many years ago.

I waited patiently for the sound that for years had warmed my heart.

Like a ray of sun bursting upon a garden, the explosion spilled under the bedroom door and into the open space.

How incredibly delightful.

The sound of two girls laughing.

Incidents

I have come to realize that I'm
not a great singer.
I'm interrupted constantly when
I try to sing.
No one would ever do that to Adele

Happenings

I have dirt under my left thumbnail all the time.

Just my left thumbnail.

That's weird, right?

Photo Ops

It's weird the way that people deal with death.

I've seen it all.

Tears of relief and warm embraces. Angry rages and family brawls over who would keep the attendance book that no one knew quite what to do with once they had it.

There are always such high emotions and queer reactions that filter around the time of someone's passing.

I'm never really caught off guard by these behaviors, with exception to one. The photo ops that have come out of these delicate occasions.

My mother, bless her heart, finds relief in photographing the stiff.

She also believes in sharing these "still life" pictures with me.

It matters not if I know the person.

It has happened on several occasions that

a stroll to the mailbox to fetch the well-intended greeting card doused in her eloquent handwriting is met with horror as I open the booby-trapped flowery letter never suspecting what lies within.

Two kittens in a basket on the outside of the card, one person in a casket on the inside.

Words of comfort concerning the deceased are included that justify, no doubt in her mind, the need to include these unwanted photos.

"Beni, the service was beautiful. Doesn't she/he look wonderful," she writes, "best he/she has looked in years!" " Wish you could have been here, love momma."

Her typical closing and sign-off is added with a flair of penmanship.

Another request goes out to stop sending me pictures of dead people!

Fast forward, years later, I'm dating a guy whose father past away.

I sent the courtesy sympathy card and made the appropriate phone calls.

As he came in the house one night for dinner he handed me a card thanking me for my kindness.

Inside was a picture of his dead dad.

Caught in a scene from the Twilight Zone he turns to me and says, "Doesn't he look wonderful?"

That's the best he's looked in years, he added.

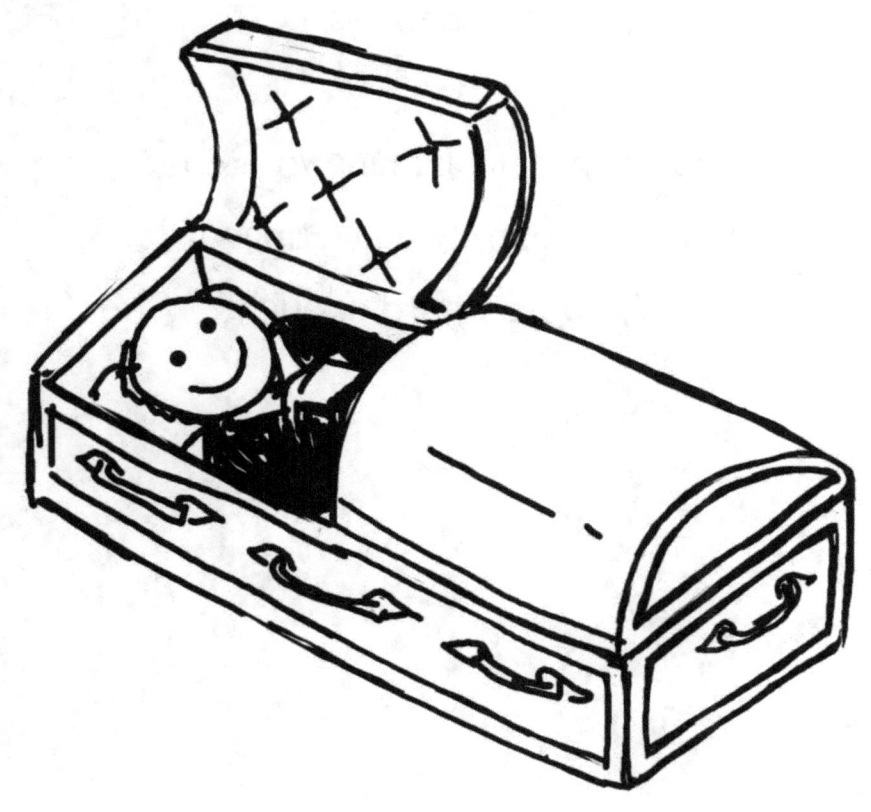

Happenings

You can make picking your toes
a hobby like knitting
if you try hard enough.

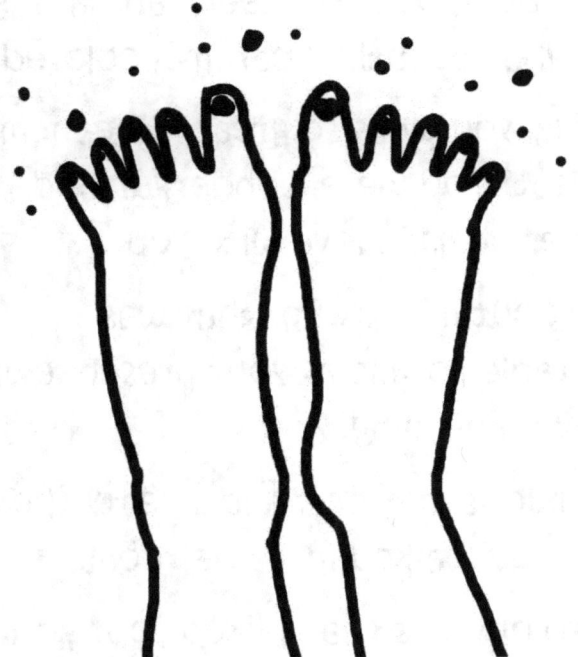

Latched

I can remember the first time I saw you sitting in my best friend's homeroom class.

My heart practically jumped out of my shirt and for the first time I was at a loss for words.

You had perfect white teeth and a huge smile. What beautiful caramel colored skin.

I felt silly, you were so great. I mean, more than great. You were wonderful, and I was head over heels in love with you.

We hung out in a group; that was comfortable for me as your presence was quite overwhelming.

I was anxious, nervous and sweaty the moment you walked into the room.

It was so obvious that I liked you. You knew it too.

I could tell you liked me as well.

You were a tower and a thin long shadow I gladly stood in.

Styx's Renegade was playing in the background when you first kissed me.

I melted like cheese. Expensive imported cheese. Not that yellow stuff.

I've never been kissed liked that. Never will again.

Our first concert was Queen. I got lost coming back to my seat. You watched me while laughing, something you later admitted.

I remember walking back and forth aimlessly.

Finally, you came down to get me and extend your long arm, which was the only thing I could see.

I latched onto you. You guided us back to our seats.

Time has passed and so have you.

Something wonderful left this planet when you did.

Sun Blocked

It doesn't take much to make me happy,

apparently for you that's not true.

Soft music. Cheap wine. Old movies, I'm
fine.

You'd rather stay home singing the blues.

I've tried to reason, maybe it's just
your season...

and not something I can undo.

But to see you smile, every once in a while,

would make my heart feel renewed.

So, go ahead and pout

work what you need out.

I'm headed to the beach.

I'll see you in a few!

Dream Big

Of all the things I wanted as a young girl, boobies had to be at the top of the "most important or I'll die" goal list.

How grueling to see the sprouting of the breast buds on other girls my age while changing in the gym locker room.

I remained flat as a board for what felt like forever.

So celebrated was the ceremonial first bra.

My consciously conservative bible beating middle class parents decided it would not be in my best interest to obtain one before "my time."

Oh, how I prayed and prayed, "Please Lord, let me grow boobies."

They did not come at age 11, 12, or 13.

At age 14 some small growth could be seen if I stood in the right light.

Everything womanish that was supposed to happen to me happened to me painfully slow.

Milestones were stretched like an elastic

band. I was considered a late bloomer.

Odd as this might sound, my boobs have a wonderful Cinderella story.

One night I went to bed and the next morning, bibbidi-bobbidi-boo, my little bitty boobies grew and grew!

No kidding.

Like Cinderella, everything changed for me once I got what I most wished for!

And Sista, I got a bumper crop!

Big, small, perky, bouncy, real, fake...it doesn't' matter.

Having boobies is powerful and fashionably fun!

So bibbidi-bobbidi-boo to each and every one!!!

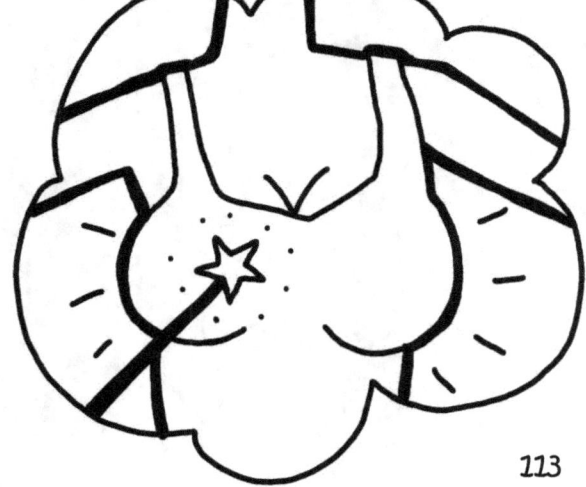

Incidents

My hair is thinning on my head, and yet
I've got the most luscious bush at
the entrance of my nose cave.

Bitch'n

The weather is warm, too warm for winter.

I peel off a scarf layer from around my neck.

The sun is so bright after a string of cloudy days.

It makes me squint and regret not wearing my sunglasses on my walk.

Irritated at the lack of communication, I try texting my daughter again.

Her preferred method of connecting.

The voice command interprets my message wrong and the editing takes me more time than mailing a handwritten letter.

I miss and step into a heaping pile of discharge from a local pup.

I grumble about reckless pet owners under my breath.

Checking the mailbox once again, I can't believe the check promised still hasn't arrived.

I climb the steps to my humble abode.

Pushing the door open
I'm welcomed by the smell
of coffee and cinnamon.
I'm reminded how lucky I am.
Silly waste of time.
All this mental bitch'n.

Left. Left. Left Right Left

The march I'm going to do today
Can't wait one day more,
Watching Ashley Judd's ranting
has shook me to my core.
The march I'm going to do today,
Can no longer be ignored.
Less talking, more action.
More loving, more traction.
More giving, just a fraction.
Going to stop writing
and head on out
That door!

Written January 21, 2017 The Women's
March on Washington

Happenings

I complimented my date on what I thought was a very

handsome picture of himself above the mantel.

It was a portrait of his mother!

Oops

Get It All Back

Knock. Knock
Who's there?
It's Me
Me Who?
The person who's heart you broke in-two
I know you are busy
But there's something I lack
And if you don't mind
I need that broken heart back
Knock. Knock
Who's There?
Me again. That's who
There are some parts that are missing
Can I borrow some glue?

Scene of the Crime.

Maximus, or Max for short, was a highly energetic lab pup that took forever to grow up!

He could leap over couches and out windows with one single bound.

He would toss himself right out of my convertible just to see if he could.

He could, and did several times.

With that much energy, it was vital that Max was walked at least twice a day.

You couldn't really call it a walk. It was more like Max dragging you at warp-speed, leaping and bounding through the upscale neighborhood that butted up to my humble abode that faced a busy bustling unwalkable street.

On one spring day, I was in a hurry to get him walked before I left for back-to-back appointments.

Dashing out the door, I forgot to grab the "all important" plastic bags that would cart dog-waste back home so I could dispose of it properly.

I wasn't worried as I'd witnessed him earlier discharging in our yard and believed I was in the clear.

After dragging me for half a mile, he stopped abruptly and assumed the position to relieve himself in front of an oversized house that boasted a manicured lawn.

"Oh no you don't," my air-deprived voice yelled out!

Dragging him by shear force another thirty yards, he backed into the woods on the far end of the property and did his business.

I kicked the expulsion farther into hiding as Max, now lighter, yanked my arm out of its socket while ramping up speed for the rest of his jaunt through the neighborhood.

I have no idea of the time that had past but it seemed like mere seconds before the road hogging Lincoln was pacing behind me.

I was finishing a thought, wondering if this car was following me when a big round-faced woman driving it pulled up beside me, maneuvering the passenger window so it was timed to my stride and framed me perfectly.

"I have something for you," she chirped.

How sweet, I thought, as I dug my heels in to get Max to slow down so I could grab the gift bag that was being extended towards me.

"You left your dog's poop in my yard," she announced.

Her smile fading quickly.

Dazed and confused I could not believe someone would actual search around in the woods for my dog's droppings, bag it, get in their car, and drive it to me like a service I had forgotten I had signed up for.

Slamming on the gas she drove off like a vapor, rolling up the window faster than I could launch the package back into her shiny leather seats.

I stood there in the road bewildered at how many times I needed someone to give me back some of my own crap. Never guessing it would happen in such a clever, unexpected way.

Max must have sensed the irony of it all. He sat perfectly still.

Panting heavily, the weight of his tongue caused his head to tilt as it spilled out the side of his mouth.

"You'll have that," his face conveyed.

Turning, he trotted off in the direction of our house as if deciding our walk had caused him too much drama and needed to end abruptly.

Passing the yard and the woods where the incident took place, I could not help but shift over close enough to the scene of the crime and do a quick investigation.

There in the same spot laid the rice peppered pile.

Evidence of Max's new diet and signature discharge.

"Elementary Dear Watson," I exclaimed in my best Sherlock Holmes voice.

I held the clutch bag up to a canine audience of one and announced, "This is not your poop!"

Cape Flapping

A prayer I've said
Every now and then
is to keep my playfulness within.
Reflecting back
On the girl I used to be
I admire her willingness to trust and believe
Determined to make
her big dreams come true...
Fearless. Unstoppable.
There was nothing she couldn't do!
Remind me kind Spirit,
whatever may become of me,
that same Skinny Beni girl
still lives inside of me!

Author: BJ Davis

B. J. Davis was born in Abilene, Texas and was raised outside of Houston. She states she was a curious child, full of energy.

"On my report card, teachers often wrote comments stating that I needed to stay in my seat and do my own work! I don't know why they thought writing that would make me actually do it.".

She's traveled the world building teams and raising the bar for leaders to be more compassionate and to practice the highest integrity with those they choose to lead. Well Known for her playful persona,, BJ Davis is the founder of Emerging Women NC that promotes and encourages inclusive leadership.

Today. she calls Raleigh, North Carolina, her home where she works, plays, writes, and consults organizations on inclusive leadership and creative play.

To book her as a speaker or trainer contact her at https://www.linkedin.com/in/brendajeandavis

Illustrator: Lidia Churakova

Lidia Churakova was born in Moscow, Russia in 1986. She studied Environmental Science at the Peoples Friendship University of Russia for two years, before moving to the USA and attending North Carolina State University. She graduated in 2012 with a Bachelor of Art and Design.

As an accomplished artist, illustrator and graphic designer Lidia has won admiration and respect for her work and creative ingenuity.

Her work can be seen downtown Raleigh where she was commissioned to help beautify one of the fastest growing cities in the country.

Known for her murals on sidewalks and buildings, her popularity and unique style has been commissioned for large and small scale projects.

She lives with her cat, Checkers in Raleigh, NC.

To see her work visit lidiachurakova.art

Created Talent Behind Skinny Beni

Creative Coach/Video Excerpt: Scott Markowitz

Www.unconstrained.me

Theme Song Writer:: Cat Albanese, "Popcorn Wings"

https://www.facebook.com/cat.albanese

Music Editing & Production: Tom Miller

https://www.facebook.com/tommiller1978

Cool Things People Would Do With Skinny Beni

"We would be outside connecting with Nature which may or may not include playing in the water, preferably in our bday-suits because, dang it, our bodies are beautiful!"
– Dr. Julie Ray

"Margaritas would be involved, and dog rescues"
–Roslind Finney

"We'd cruise and if Heart came on we'd turn it up to ear drum bursting decibels. and we'd also form a pack never letting anything or anyone come between our friendship."
– Vicky Howard

"Skinny Beni and I would explore the Universe looking for new and fun adventures!"
–Ann Jagger

"Google Troy Bilski"
– Merrillee Jacobson

"We'd go dumpster diving while everyone else is at work and we'd find really cool stuff."

– Lisa Bald

"Light some smoke, maybe drink some tea, and she'd be my plus-one at Tinker Bell's (real name Jessica) wedding."

– Araina Nolls

"Skinny Beni and I would go camping and sit by the campfire stuffing our cheeks with marshmallows, sing campfire songs and ending the night with staring at the stars that shine like fireflies."

– Tina Markowitz

"Dink wine!" "That's what Skinny Beni and I would do if we were best friends."

– William Ramey

"If Skinny Beni and I were best friends, we would people watch."

– Kristin Hartzell

www.ingramcontent.com/pod-product-compliance
Lightning Source LLC
Chambersburg PA
CBHW070045260626
47159CB00005B/2132